This book belongs to

For Mum, Dad and Ade,
with love
K.S.

For Ivan, who was always there
kicking in my belly
D.K.

First published in 2011 in Great Britain by

Gullane Children's Books

185 Fleet Street, London EC4A 2HS
www.gullanebooks.com

This paperback edition first published in 2012.

1   3   5   7   9   10   8   6   4   2

Text © Karen Saunders 2011
Illustrations © Dubravka Kolanovic 2011

The right of Karen Saunders and Dubravka Kolanovic to be identified as the author and illustrator of
this work has been asserted by them in accordance with the Copyright, Designs and Patents Act, 1988.

A CIP record for this title is available from the British Library.

ISBN: 978-1-86233-824-1

Printed and bound in China

Baby Badger's Wonderful Night

Karen Saunders • Dubravka Kolanovic

GULLANE
CHILDREN'S BOOKS

At the end of the day, the sun slipped away behind the hills.
Papa Badger and Baby Badger watched as the
light faded and darkness crept towards them.
Baby Badger shivered and began to feel afraid.

'I don't like the night,' Baby Badger whispered.
Papa Badger took him by the hand.
'There's no need to be frightened,' he said.
'The night is wonderful. Let me show you.'

It was very dark inside the wood.
'It's too black and scary,' Baby Badger said,
snuggling nearer to Papa Badger.

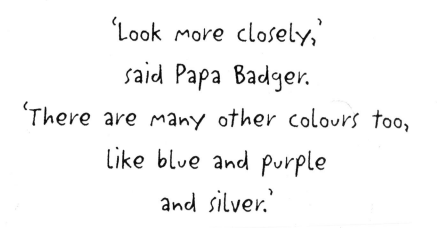

'Look more closely,'
said Papa Badger.
'There are many other colours too,
like blue and purple
and silver.'

Baby Badger saw all the colours
of the night and felt a bit better.

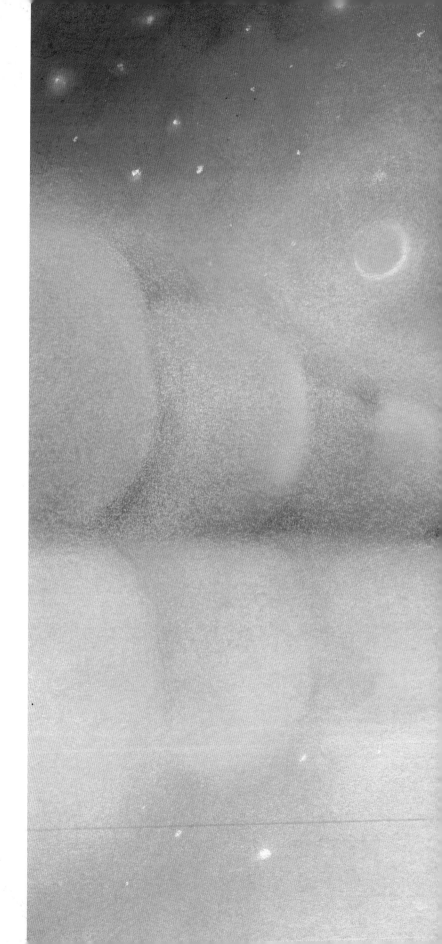

Up in the sky,
tiny stars were sparkling.
'Why do they shine?'
asked Baby Badger.
'They light up the night,'
said Papa Badger,
'and stop us feeling alone.'

Baby Badger gazed at the stars,
which twinkled back at him.

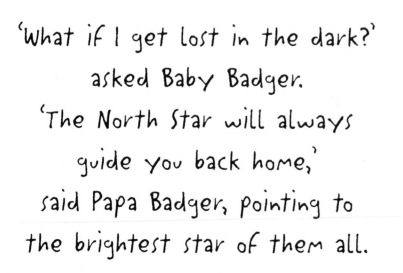

'What if I get lost in the dark?'
asked Baby Badger.
'The North Star will always
guide you back home,'
said Papa Badger, pointing to
the brightest star of them all.

Baby Badger looked
at the shining star and
knew he was safe.

Suddenly, above their heads, a shooting star lit up the sky.

'Quickly! Close your eyes and make a wish,' said Papa Badger.

Baby Badger squeezed his eyes shut and wished very hard.

'Now do you see that there's no need
to be afraid?' said Papa Badger.
Baby Badger yawned and
cuddled up next to him.
'The night is magical,' he murmured.
'It's full of stars and colours and wishes.'

Away in the distance,
the first rays of morning were spreading across the fields.
Next to Papa Badger, Baby Badger felt safe and warm.
Slowly, his eyes closed.

'Come on, little one,' Papa Badger said softly.
'It's time to go home.'
He scooped Baby Badger into his arms . . .

and carried him back through the wood to bed.